Thumbelina is Dead

and

Why I Broke Up With My Boyfriends

Stories and Artwork by
Tonya Smith-Duncan

Digital Artwork Editing by Tone Lorenza

Printed in the United States of America

GoToPublish LLC
1-888-337-1724
www. Gotopublish. Com
info@gotopublish. Com

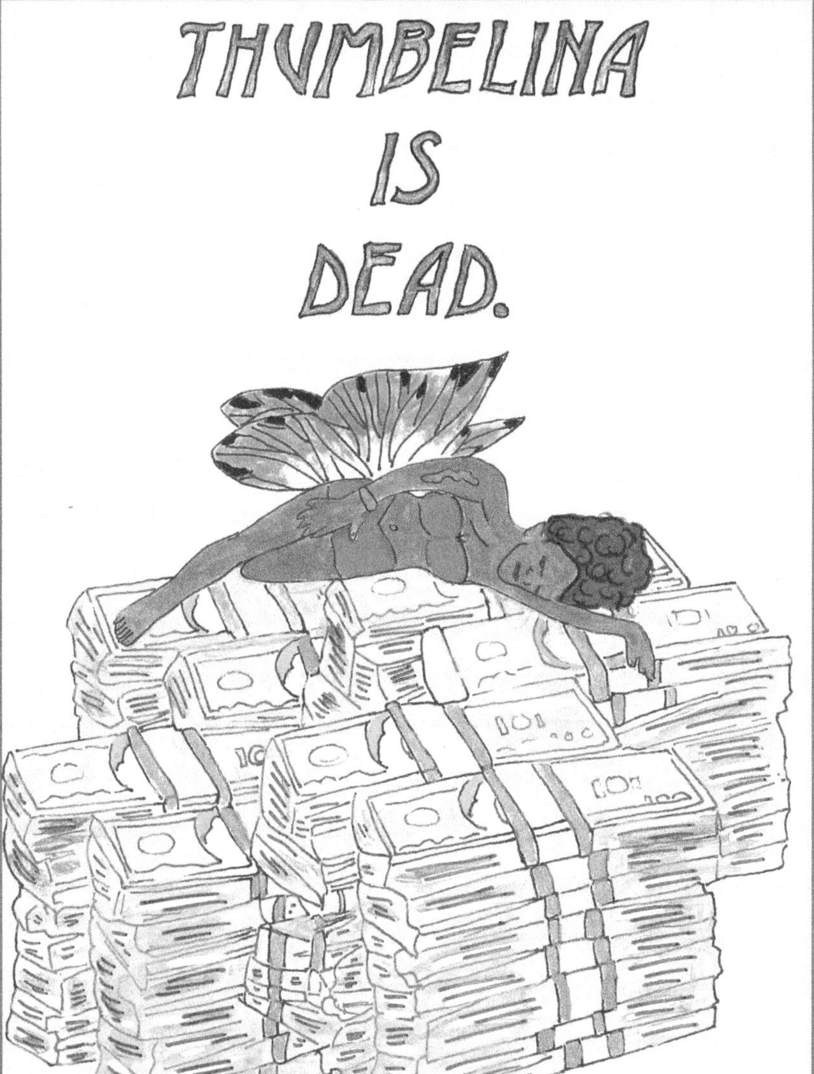
THUMBELINA
IS
DEAD.
By
Sonya Smith-Bauer

I DON'T BELIEVE IN FAIRY TALES. IN FACT, I'M TOO AWARE OF THE OPPOSITE.

REALITIES.

I TRY TO MAKE THEM PRETTY - WITH MONEY. CAPITALIZING ON OTHER PEOPLE'S REALITIES IS MY SPECIALTY.

I'M MAIA.

I GIVE LOANS. SMALL ONES. BIG ONES.

NECESSARY ONES.

THE PEOPLE, THEY FIND ME.

MOSTLY WOMEN THOUGH.

THEY ALWAYS PAY ME BACK.

WITH 40% INTEREST, OF COURSE.

MY FIRST CLIENT WAS A FRIEND OF MINE THAT HAD A GAMBLING PROBLEM. DENISE. SHE GOT INTO A HOLE WITH THE RENT.

HER HUBBY GAVE IT TO HER TO PAY, AND SHE SPENT IT.

FLOYD SHOWED ME HOW. HE WAS THE LOVE OF MY LIFE.

SO I BORROWED IT FROM FLOYD AND THREW IN A FINDER'S FEE FOR MYSELF.

HE SHOWED ME HOW TO HANDLE HER: I THREATENED TO TELL HER HUSBAND ABOUT THE GAMBLING AND HER FUCKING A SECURITY GUARD AT THE CASINO.

IT ALL WORKED OUT IN THE END.

I LIKE TO HELP.

AFTER ALL, WE NEED TO HAVE GOALS.

I BELIEVE IN THAT.

Tonya Smith-Duncan

YOU KNOW WHAT I SEE?

WOMEN ALWAYS MESS UP OVER LOVE. IT'S THEIR BAD HABIT.

MEN, OVER POWER.

BOTH WANT MORE THAN THEY CAN FINANCIALLY GET. (MISGUIDED GOALS.)

THE STORIES REPEAT THEMSELVES OVER AND OVER.
NOW, I DON'T BELIEVE IN FAIRY TALES, BUT I DO BELIEVE IN LOVE.

I'M ALWAYS WILLING TO HELP OTHERS OUT AS LONG AS THEY HAVE A JOB. OR INCOME.

FOR EXAMPLE...

ONE GUY NAMED SHANE THAT I KNEW FELL IN LOVE WITH A CHICK IN A CATHOUSE.

HE WAS A MECHANIC, BUT HIS WIFE MADE MORE MONEY THAN HE DID AFTER HE STARTED CHASING THAT HOE.

HENCE, HE BORROWED FROM ME SO HIS PEOPLE WOULD NOT KNOW.

ALWAYS PAID ME BACK ON TIME THOUGH.

THAT STOPPED AFTER HE GAVE HIS WIFE THE CLAP.

SHE TRIED TO KILL SHANE AND THE HOE.

SO SORRY 'BOUT THAT.

ONE GIRL NAMED TISH I DO SOME BUSINESS WITH JUST SHOPS TOO DAMNED MUCH.

HER CREDIT CARD DEBTS ARE MASSIVE. THAT IS HER BAD, BAD HABIT.

OH, AND PARTYING.

IN BETWEEN HER SUGAR DADDIES, SHE ALWAYS RUNS OUT OF MONEY.

TISH, THE TRUST FUND CHILD. (WHOSE NOT A CHILD.)

USED TO BE A DANCER. PRETTY GIRL, BUT DUMB LIKE A ROCK WITH MONEY.

I'M EXPECTING HER ANY DAY NOW.

SOME PEOPLE THINK I'M GENEROUS,

BUT I AM NOT.
THIS GUY NAMED MANNY FOUND ME ONCE. DON'T KNOW HOW.

HE SAID HE WAS A FILMMAKER.
HE WANTED ME TO "INVEST" IN HIS PROJECT.
MY PSYCHE TOLD ME NOT TO, NO MATTER HOW

CONVINCING HE SOUNDED.

I LISTEN TO MY GUT. I DON'T CARE WHOSE MOUTH IS MOVING.

TRUST ME!

NO.

MY DECISION WAS QUITE SIMPLE.

HE TALKED A GOOD GAME, BUT HE DIDN'T HAVE AN INCOME TO FINANCE HIS DREAMS AND BACK THE LOAN UP.

THE GAMBLER'S WOMAN
BY MANNY ROSS

THAT WASN'T MY PROBLEM AND I WASN'T GOING TO LET IT BE.
(ALSO, HIS SCRIPT SUCKED.)

THAT'S NOT HOW I DO CHARITY, BABY.
TO ME, THAT WOULD BE THROWING MONEY TO THE WIND.
I TOLD YOU...

...I DON'T BELIEVE IN FAIRY TALES.

8

SOME TIME AGO, MY NEIGHBOR'S DAUGHTER, OLEAN, GOT KNOCKED UP IN COLLEGE, A SWEET KID, SHE IS.

SHE ONLY HAD HALF THE DUCKETS TO GET RID OF IT, AND COULDN'T ASK HER MOM FOR THE REST.

I HAD TO THINK ABOUT IT, BUT I LOANED OLEAN THE DIFFERENCE ANYWAY.

DRUNK PARTIERS. A NAMELESS FACE AND A ONE-NIGHT STAND. KIDS DO CARELESS THINGS. (I'VE BEEN ONE.)

OLEAN HAD SOME LITTLE JOB AT SCHOOL, BUT HAD A HARD TIME SAVING FOR BIG THINGS. SHE WAS SUCH A GOOD KID, I ONLY CHARGED HER 30%

(PLUS, SHE CRIED.)

OLEAN PAID ME BACK PROMPTLY AND SHE GRADUATED WITH HONORS.

HER MOM WAS NONE THE WISER AND VERY PROUD OF HER.   (I CRIED.)

HAVE I EVER BEEN IN A JAM? NOT TOO OFTEN. I MAKE GOOD DECISIONS AND HAVE A LUCKY TOUCH WITH THE FUNDS.

AND I HAVE A VERY SIMPLE PLAN— I DON'T LOAN A NICKEL THE FIRST IF YOU DON'T HAVE INCOME BECAUSE THEN YOU WON'T PAY ME MY MONEY.

THEN, I'M GONNA HAVE TO HURT YOU.

OR SHOOT YOU.

OR BOTH.

OR GET BEANZIE TO DO IT 'CAUSE I DON'T ENJOY THAT SHIT. JUST THE LOOT. AND GETTING THINGS DONE.

COMMON SENSE,

RIGHT?

WAIT A MINUTE.
I TAKE THAT BACK. ONCE, I FELL FOR A DUDE WHO WAS RIDICULOUSLY BAD LUCK.

(BUT HE WAS HOT.)

Tonya Smith-Duncan

I REMEMBER WHILE I WAS DATING KOLT, I BEGAN TO HAVE PROBLEMS WITH THIS KNOT-HEADED CHICK NAMED ADDY.

I STILL DON'T KNOW IF SHE AND KOLT WERE DOUBLE-CROSSING ME OR WHAT.

BUT THAT STUPID GIRL...

...GOT IT IN HER HEAD THAT SHE DIDN'T WANT TO PAY ME BACK MY DOUGH. SHE FELL TWO WEEKS BEHIND. I WAS N̲O̲T̲ ENCHANTED.

THIS WAS AFTER I LOANED HER TO FIX HER A CAR SO SHE TO WORK. I GAVE SHE HAD TWO KIDS TO

$2,000 PIECE OF COULD GET BECAUSE FEED. SEE WHERE I SCREWED UP? I MADE IT MY PROBLEM.

DAMN, SHE PISSED ME OFF.! SO I GOT BEANZIE TO SHOOT HER IN THE FOOT.

NOT THE DRIVING FOOT, OF COURSE. BITCH HAD TO GO TO WORK YOU KNOW, AND GET MY MONEY.

WITHIN A WEEK OUT OF THE HOSPITAL, SHE PAID ME BACK. WITH MY 40% INTEREST, OF COURSE

(CHEERS.)

AFTER THAT, I GOT RID OF KOLT AS FAST AS RAIN COULD RUN.

I NEVER HAD ANOTHER PROBLEM WITH MY MONEY AGAIN.

REALITY.

(SNAP.)

AND VICE VERSA.

I'VE SEEN PLENTY OF GOLDEN GIRLS LOSE THEIR SHINE BY JUST LOVING THE WRONG MAN.

IT'S A CHAIN REACTION AS OLD AS TIME.

Tonya Smith-Duncan

BELIEVE ME, I KNOW WHAT A TREASURE IT IS TO LOVE A GOOD DUDE.

IT JUST DOESN'T HAPPEN A LOT.

FLOYD TAUGHT ME THAT; EVEN THOUGH HE GOT ME INTO THIS LOAN-SHARK-THING IN A MINOR WAY.

MY FLOYD WAS AS POWERFUL AS THEY COME.

FLOYD. HE MADE ME LOVE HIM BEFORE I FOUND OUT WHAT HE WAS DOING TO ME. SNEAKY, THAT WAS.

SWEPT ME OFF MY FEET.

I TELL YOU,

I STOPPED MODELING AND PARTYING AND FOLLOWED FLOYD EVERY WHERE.

I CRAVED HIM AND KISSED THE GROUND HE WALKED ON — REGARDLESS OF HOW HE GOT MONEY.

PEOPLE TOLD ME THAT HE WAS EVIL.
 I SAW IT IN HIS FACE SOMETIMES, LIKE...

...WHEN HE WAS PISSED WITH SOMEONE ABOUT THE MONEY NOT ROLLING RIGHT.

I ASKED HIM ONCE IF HE EVER KILLED ANYONE BUT FLOYD NEVER ANSWERED. HE JUST IGNORED THE INQUIRY, THEN KISSED AND DISMISSED ME.

IT WAS NOT A PROBLEM, BUT TO ME IT'S STILL A MYSTERY.

SORRY TO TELL YOU, THAT GANGSTER WAS ALWAYS GOOD TO ME.

FLOYD IS DEAD. HE GOT SHOT BY SOMEONE WHO COULDN'T PAY HIM BACK AND OUT ON FLIPPED HIM.

THEN THE PUNK TURNED THE GUN ON HIMSELF. THAT DAY I GUESS, FLOYD'S MOJO WASN'T WORKING OUT.

A PIECE OF ME DIED. I REMEMBER IT LIKE IT WAS YESTERDAY. I'LL NEVER LOVE LIKE THAT AGAIN. I KNOW IT.

ANYWAY, BECAUSE WE HAD NO KIDS OR KIN, FLOYD LEFT ME ALL OF HIS MONEY, BEANZIE HIS BODYGUARD, AND A KNOW-HOW FOR THE BUSINESS.

WILL

I INVESTED THE CASH, AND I NEVER HAD TO WORK AGAIN. EXCEPT THIS "HELPING" THING.

...BECAUSE I LIKE IT. GOD BLESS MY FLOYD, WHEREVER HE IS RIGHT NOW.

IT'S BEEN FIVE YEARS, BUT I STILL MISS HIM. I LOOK FOR HIM IN EVERY GUY I MEET, BUT I JUST DON'T SEE HIM, OR FEEL HIM. I GUESS I HAVEN'T REALLY MOVED ON YET.

I TRIED THOUGH.

TWO YEARS AGO, I TOOK A BREAK AND WENT SOUTH TO SEE MY MOM WHEN SHE GOT ILL.

ACCIDENTALLY, I FELL FOR A RED-BONED GUY DOWN THERE WHO HAD NO IDEA WHAT MY LIFESTYLE WAS.

(COUNTRY, FAMILY-FARM BOY RYAN.)

IT WAS SWEET AND THE SEX WAS WHOLESOME. LIKE VISITING MY YOUTH ALL OVER AGAIN.

CARING ABOUT LOVE, AND TREES AND CLOUDS AND GOOD SHIT LIKE THAT. LIVING IN A CITY, YOU CAN LOSE TOUCH.

BUT I KNEW I HAD TO LET RYAN GO.

HE HAD TOO MANY STARS IN HIS EYES AND NO CLUE OF HOW TO TOUCH THE SKY.

SO...

..WHEN MOM GOT WELL, I HAD BEANZIE COME AND GET ME. I JUMPED IN THE CAR IN THE MIDDLE OF THE NIGHT...

...AND RETURNED TO THE CITY WITHOUT SAYING GOODBYE.

WE WEREN'T COMPATIBLE, RYAN AND I BUT IT WAS NICE WHILE IT LASTED.

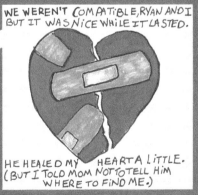

HE HEALED MY HEART A LITTLE. (BUT I TOLD MOM NOT TO TELL HIM WHERE TO FIND ME.)

RIGHT NOW, MY MAIN HONEY-MAN'S NAME IS ALAN. HE'S A LAWYER; ISN'T THAT FUNNY? CORPORATE, NOT CRIMINAL. HE'S QUITE A SHARK, I MIGHT ADD. MY TYPE.(1 OF THEM)

WE'VE BEEN TOGETHER A GOOD MINUTE. I MET HIM AT A JAZZY RESTAURANT DOING LUNCH.

TO PICK ME UP, HE SENT ME A GOOD GLASS OF RED WINE ALONG WITH HIS PHONE NUMBER.

AL KNOWS WHAT I DO. HE FOUND OUT ACCIDENTALLY DURING A TRANSACTION. THAT WAS URGENT.

HE THINKS WHAT I DO IS "CUTE." MAYBE BABY...

...BUT IN THIS ARENA, I'M WAY SMARTER THAN YOU.

TO STAY ON EVERYONE, JUGGLE TOP OF AND TO 3 TO 4

DESPERADOS, YOU HAVE CERTAIN KIND A WEEK, TO HAVE A OF SOMETHING THAT'S TWO STEPS AHEAD. I'M NOT UNDERDOG, AND IT HAS TO BE DONE.

YOU CAN CALL THAT CUTE IF YOU WANT TO, BUT I WOULDN'T.

I LIKE ALAN A LOT. THE SEX IS GREAT BUT I DON'T LOVE HIM. HE ARGUES THAT I DON'T LET HIM GET CLOSE TO ME...

...BUT I JUST WON'T USE THAT WORD BETWEEN US. BESIDES, I'VE GOT OTHERS.

I DON'T LIKE IT STIRS UP. TO MIX POTS; BAD THINGS

I HAVE TO BECAUSE DOESN'T DO THIS I KNOW HE UNDERSTAND...

... MY
REALITY.
I'M A HEATHEN AND I LOVE IT.
I DRINK, I GAMBLE, AND I FUCK.
AND NOT NECESSARILY IN
THAT ORDER.
   I'M NOT THE GIRL NEXT DOOR AND
I'M NOT TRYING TO BE EITHER.

I LOVE TO HELP OUT.

ESPECIALLY IF THERE'S A
DOLLAR TO ADD UP.

I LOVE MY MEN AND I LOVE
MY LOT. I DON'T WANT TO CHANGE,
THANK YOU.

NO BULL, NO CRAP TO RECOUNT.
ALL TRUTH. ALL GAIN. I THINK
ALAN LIKES THAT, THE HONESTY.

WHAT HE DOES KNOW HASN'T
HURT HIM SO FAR.

KNOW WHAT I MEAN?

THINGS ARE ALWAYS ROLLING. FOR INSTANCE, RIGHT NOW, I'M HELPING CALLY OUT.

SHE'S DATING A BOXER, BABY BOY BRYAN, WHO'S ABSOLUTELY, FINANCIALLY, OUT OF HER LEAGUE. HE TAKES HER TO SO MANY EVENTS AND UNFORTUNATELY, SHE HAS TO KEEP UP APPEARANCES. IF SHE DOESN'T, CALLY THINKS SHE'S OUT OF THE GAME. (SHE JUST MIGHT BE.) MONEY-WISE, HE'S A GREAT BOYFRIEND AND ALL...

...WHEN HE REMEMBERS TO BE.

BUT IN BETWEEN HIS BEING SO GENEROUS TO HER, I GET LEANED ON BY CALLY. WHEN B. FINDS OUT, HE PAYS ME BACK...

...EVEN MY FEE. HE'S COOL LIKE THAT. SO CALLY IS OKAY WITH ME.

PLUS, BABY BOY'S FRIENDS ARE RICH, FASCINATING, AND VERY BECOMING TO MY EYES.

(AND, ON TOP OF ALL-ACCESS BETTING, I GET INTO THE FIGHTS FOR FREE.)

I DON'T HAVE A LOT OF FRIENDS; I JUST KNOW A LOT OF PEOPLE. I ONLY HAVE BEANZIE AND MY BEST FRIEND LOANDA, REALLY.

(BRF!)

BEANZIE IS SO CLOSE TO ME THAT HE SOMETIMES SLEEPS IN MY BED WITH ME. WE DON'T FUCK. IT'S JUST FOR SECURITY. HEY, I DON'T BLAME HIM.

MY BED IS EXPENSIVELY COZY.

LOANDA, I HELP OUT PERIODICALLY. SHE'S GREAT — NOTHING LIKE ME.

PERFECTLY ON THE UP-AND-UP.

WE GO WAY BACK TO HIGH SCHOOL.

SHE HAD DREAMS ~ SHE WENT TO COLLEGE FOR FASHION DESIGN, BUT DROPPED OUT TO GO WORK FOR A FAMOUS DESIGNER. SHE LEARNED A LOT FROM HIM.

BUT, LO'S VERY TALENTED, ACTUALLY.

SHE STAYED WITH HIM FOR 6 YEARS.

HE ONLY FIRED HER BECAUSE SHE SCREWED HIS BOYFRIEND. (HA!)

AFTERWARDS, LO CAME TO ME, WANTING A LOAN FOR A BOUTIQUE. I THOUGHT IT WAS A GOOD INVESTMENT. SHE PAID ME BACK EVERY DIME WITHIN 2 MONTHS OF OPENING.

WITH MY INTEREST, OF COURSE.

LO'S

BECAUSE I KNEW HER SO LONG, I ONLY CHARGED HER 20%. MY GIRL. I NEVER HAD TO SHOOT HER OR ANYTHING.

BEANZIE'S NOT A SLAVE, YOU KNOW. I PAY HIM HANDSOMELY.

(IT WAS IN THE WILL.)

WANT TO KNOW A SECRET ABOUT HIM?

HIS EYES ARE MAGIC; THEY ALWAYS CHANGE COLOR. IT'S STRANGE, BUT IT'S COOL TO SEE.

ONLY GOD KNOWS WHAT WAS GOING ON UP IN THAT FAMILY TREE...

...TO INHERIT A TRAIT LIKE THAT.

CHICKS LOVE IT. YOU SHOULD HEAR HIS CRAZY GIRLFRIEND STORIES.

THEY ALWAYS MAKE ME LAUGH.

BEANZIE'S GOOD FOR ME. SOMETIMES, I GET WOUND UP SO TIGHT ABOUT LIFE, THAT ONLY HE CAN SOOTHE ME.

WHEN I NEED HIM, HE'S THERE,

THAT'S FOR SURE. LOYALTY AND LOVE SOMETIMES GO HAND-IN-HAND.

WE HAVE A BOND-THROUGH MY LLOYD, AND TIME. AND WE HAVE A LIFESTYLE.

BEANZIE PROTECTS THAT.

HIS GIRLFRIENDS NEVER UNDERSTAND, SO HE DOESN'T EXPLAIN ME TO THEM ANYMORE.

(TALK TO THE HAND BEANZIE!)

BEANZIE'S KIND OF PRIVATE.

BETWEEN YOU AND ME? I TRUST BEANZIE WITH MY MONEY...

...AND MY LIFE. BUT I KNOW I WOULDN'T PUSH FATE.

THUMBELINA WAS A FAIRY WITH NO WINGS AND BORN NO BIGGER THAN A THUMB.

MOM TOLD ME THIS STORY... ...WHEN I WAS VERY YOUNG.

BEFORE I KNEW MY WAY AROUND LIFE, LOVE AND MEN, AND BEFORE I KNEW HOW PEOPLE COULD GET IN SO MUCH TROUBLE OVER A DIME.

HER MOTHER WISHED FOR HER AND IT WAS GRANTED. YEP, BORN FROM A WISH AND A FLOWER.

THUMBELINA WAS SO PRETTY THAT UGLY THINGS IN LIFE KEPT KIDNAPPING HER.

SHE FINALLY ESCAPED WITH A SWALLOW SHE WAS KIND TO. SHE SAVED ITS LIFE,

TWICE, SHE GOT AWAY. (WITH HELP, OF COURSE.)

SO IT SAVED HERS. THEY HAD THAT EXCHANGE FROM THE KINDNESS OF THEIR HEARTS.

THAT SWALLOW FLEW HER FAR AWAY FROM THE UGLY THINGS AND BROUGHT HER TO THE KING OF THE FAIRIES WHO WAS AS BEAUTIFUL AS SHE WAS. (SURPRISE, SURPRISE.)

HE LOVED HER AND EVEN GAVE HER WINGS AND CHANGED HER NAME TO MINE: MAI'A.

(DID I MENTION THAT SHE COULD ALSO SING?)

THE POINT IS: IF THUMBELINA HADN'T BEEN RESCUED, HER LIFE WOULD HAVE BEEN UGLY AND VERY DIFFICULT. NOW, WE ALL KNOW THAT THUMBELINA SHIT ISN'T REAL.

AND, THE STORY WAS BORN SO LONG AGO, THAT IF SHE WERE REAL, SHE'D BE DEAD.

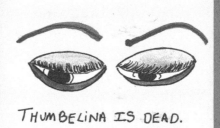

YEAH.

THUMBELINA IS DEAD.

'KINDNESS-FROM-THE-HEART' MY ASS; THOSE DAYS WERE A LONG, LONG, TIME AGO.

I LEARNED AS I GOT OLDER, YOU HAVE TO PAY PEOPLE TO RESCUE YOU! UNLESS YOU'RE A HUMANITARIAN.

WHICH I AM NOT.

SO, PAY ME.

WHAT'S RIGHT IS RIGHT.

WHY I BROKE UP WITH MY BOY-FRIENDS.

(BY
Janyt Smith)

(1) I DIDN'T LIKE THE WAY HE SMELLED AFTER SEX.

(2) HE CHEATED ON ME WHEN HE DIDN'T HAVE TO.

(3) HE HATED <u>MY</u> FRIENDS.

(4) I HATED _HIS_ FRIENDS.

(5) HE WAS IN MY FACE *TOO* MUCH AND *WAY* TOO NEEDY.

(6) HE DIDN'T PAY ENOUGH ATTENTION TO ME.

(7) HE SNORED TOO LOUD.

(8) HE STOOD ME UP. *TWICE.*

(9) HE SCARED ME.

(10) HE WAS AN UGLY SLEEPER, AND UGLY WHEN HE WOKE UP IN THE MORNING.

(11)HE DID *TOO* MANY DRUGS.

(12) HE DIDN'T DRINK. NOT EVEN <u>WINE</u>!

(13) I REALIZED HE WAS LAZY.

(14) HE WORKED TOO DAMN MUCH.

(15) ENTERTAINING HE WAS, BUT I DIDN'T BELIEVE A DAMN WORD HE SAID.

(17) HE WENT AWAY AND I DIDN'T WANT TO WAIT.

(18) SEX WITH HIM PUT ME IN THE H-O-S-P-I-T-A-L. (Don't ask.)

(19) HE TRIED TO KILL ME.

(20) HE PULLED OUT HAND PUPPETS ON ME.

(21) HE ALWAYS TRIED TO "OVERRIDE" ME.

(22) HE HAD <u>ZERO</u> BACKBONE; NEVER STOOD UP FOR HIMSELF.

(23) HE WAS TOO POOR (AND DIDN'T TRY TO CHANGE IT).

(24) HE WAS TOO RICH (I COULDN'T KEEP UP).

(25) HE WASN'T LUCKY.

(26) HE LIKED TO BE ILLEGAL.

(27) I HATED HIS FAMILY.

(28) HE GAVE ME AN ULTIMATUM; I CHOSE TO LEAVE.

(29) HE STAYED TOO DAMN CLOSE WITH HIS EX.

(30) HE HAD MORE KIDS THAN ME.

(31) HE WOULD RATHER BE IN A BAR THAN BE WITH ME.

(32) HE WAS NOT A SPORTS LOVER- HE WAS A SPORTS *FANATIC!*

(33) HE COULDN'T S-P-E-L-L.

(34) I REALIZED HE WAS A SLOB.

(35) HE LIVED TOO FAR AWAY.

(36) FUN, BUT TOO CHILDISH.

(37) CUTE AS CUPCAKE-BEEFCAKE, BUT DUMBER THAN A BAG O' ROCKS.

(38) SO EDUCATED, HE THOUGHT HE WAS SMARTER THAN ME.

(39) HE WAS VERY, <u>VERY</u> STINGY.

(40) HE FUCKING KNEW EVERYTHING.

(41) HE COULDN'T SAY NO TO HIS FRIENDS & FAMILY AND GAVE AWAY EVERY NICKEL HE GOT.

(42) UGLY TEMPER. AND, OVER THE _STUPIDEST_ SHIT IN THE WORLD.

(43) HE COULDN'T FIX SHIT-JUST PLAIN USELESS.

(44) HE ABANDONED ME WHEN I WAS SICK.

(45) LIFE HAPPENED; HE GOT VERY DEPRESSED.

(46) HE WAS SO CRAZY, I CHANGED MY MIND.

(47) HE/THEY ADMITTED THEY HAD BEEN "COMMITTED".

(48) HE LET ME DOWN.